The Hen House Chronicles

By

Sue Carlton Swinson

Contents

Miss Ina Mae

The old house stood on a hill overlooking the small town of Jenkinsville. It had stood there for over a hundred years. It was called "the old Jenkins place" by the town's people. As a matter of fact, Miss Ina Mae Jenkins still lives there. Although the Jenkins fortune has long been gone, Miss Ina Mae is afforded all the respect and honor of an era person by everyone. To this sleepy little hamlet, Miss Jenkins is their special person.

Miss Ina Mae taught school to most of the town folks and most of their children. She was well into her seventies when she retired. She also sang in the Methodist Church choir for so many years no one could count them.

Still standing tall and with a carriage that belies her age, she is still greeted by everyone when she gets into her old Hudson car and goes into town.

She drives in the middle of the road, and is so slow
there is no real danger. The town folks just pull over
and wave as she drives by at a break-neck speed of
thirty miles an hour.

The Hudson car itself brings as much attention
as Miss Ina Mae. It looks like it just rolled off the
showroom floor. It is a 1940 Hudson Deluxe. It is
black with lots of shiny chrome and wonderful wide
whitewall tires. The interior is immaculate. It is
beautiful. Joe at the garage drools when she brings
it in for the car's annual tune-up. It is the perfect car
for Miss Ina Mae.

Miss Ina Mae still wears ankle length dresses,
gloves, sensible shoes and hose, and a hat, straw
or felt depending on the season of year. When she
parks in front of Wag-a-Sack grocery strangers in
town stop, stare and smile. She looks like she just
drove in from another era.

Everyone has their own story about Miss Ina
Mae. This one is about the time the Jenkins County
highway supervisors, Homer Hawkins and Cecil
Johnson, came out to inform her that the county was
going to take a corner of her land to widen the road.

When the two gentlemen arrived, Miss Ina Mae
was working in her flower beds.

"Good morning, Miss Ina Mae," said Homer.

"It is sure a fine spring day. I bet you are going to have some real pretty flowers this summer." He smiled. He called it politicking, but that is not what it was. It was…well, you fill in the blanks.

Cecil murmured, "Mornin."

Homer continued. "Mighty pretty place you have here. The lilac bushes are just full of blooms. Yes sir, mighty pretty place."

"Good morning, Homer. Cecil. Yes, it is a fine day. What brings you out this way?"

"Well, Miss Ina Mae, we came out to discuss a proposition with you. The county is going to widen this intersection at the corner of your land. We want to take about an acre of your land to do that. I am sure you would be pleased to do that for the county." Homer was smiling and rubbing his hands together.

Looking him straight in the eyes she said, "No, Homer, I would not be "pleased" to do that. There is no discussion. No such thing is going to happen to the Jenkins land."

"Miss Ina Mae…" began Cecil. One look from Miss Ina Mae and he shut his mouth.

"Now, Miss Ina Mae, let's just see if we can work this out." Homer smiled, as most politicians do, especially with elderly people; very condescending like.

"Homer, you or no one else is going to take one inch of my land today or ever. Now, excuse me, and be on your way. Our business is concluded. Good day." She turned back to her flower beds.

"Miss Ina Mae, don't make this hard." Homer put a little plea in his voice. "The county can take the land if it has a mind. We don't want to do that. We're friends. So…" Homer chuckled under his breath.

The threat was presented and received. The line had been drawn. Waterloo was very close at hand.

Again, she politely said, "No."

Homer cleared his throat to speak. She interrupted him.

"Excuse me, MR. Hawkins. I'll be right back." Miss Ina Mae went into the house and returned with her daddy's old shotgun.

"Now Homer," she spoke with deadly calm, "you were stupid in school and you still are. You never listen to instructions. Now, I must ask you and Cecil to leave. Get off my land! Good day."

"Miss Ina Mae…Miss Ina Mae." Homer said, backing toward the truck. Cecil was already way out in front of him.

Miss Ina Mae pulled the hammer back on that old gun, then lifted it to her shoulder. Just as Homer dived into the driver's side of the truck and Cecil dived into the other, she pulled the trigger.

She missed everything, but the lilac bush by the driveway. There was a storm of raining purple blossoms, as Miss Ina Mae pulled the hammer back on the other barrel and prepared to fire again.

By this time Homer has the truck started, is grinding gears and jumping off the clutch so quickly it dies. Poor Cecil is screaming.

This time she takes careful aim, and as Homer finally gets the truck in gear and fishtails toward the main road, she pulls the trigger and blows out the rear window. Homer and Cecil both scream and Cecil dives into the floor board. Homer guns the truck and slings gravel and sand as they leave the driveway.

"Huh, I think I need target practice." Miss Ina Mae said, with her hand covering her mouth in disbelief. "I was aiming for the back tire!"

To say the least, the Jenkins place never lost a foot of ground, unless you count the gravel and sand Homer slung leaving. After the townspeople heard what happened, Homer and Cecil both lost the upcoming election. Folks really do love Miss Ina Mae.

Uncle Spooky and No Quittin' Sense.

This story is about Aunt Lurlene and Uncle Spooky. I do not know his name. He has always been called "Spooky" and since he is my papa's brother, it just follows that we kids would call him Uncle Spooky.

Uncle Spooky was the kind of person who thought a constant barrage of practical jokes was funny to everyone. No matter how often he had been asked to stop this nonsense, he never listened. He was manic about practical jokes, but he finally learned his lesson and that is my story.

Aunt Lurlene was a lady who worried about everything: grocery prices at the A & P, if the hens would lay, uprising in Bongo-Bongo… and the list could go on. Any story she heard, she re-told with great negative exaggerations. She was also superstitious and afraid of any little noise.

One Saturday night Agnes and Turner, Aunt Lurlene's sister and her husband, came over for supper and dominoes. It was a fun night until Uncle Spooky deliberately turned the conversation to ghosts, spirits, voodoo and anything supernatural. This unnerved Aunt Lurlene completely. Uncle Spooky kidded her about it.

After a long evening of dominoes, chocolate cake, green Jell-O and coffee, Aunt Agnes and Uncle Turner decided it was time to go home. With hugs and good-byes, Aunt Agnes and Uncle Turner roared off into the night in their old pick-up truck, the One-eyed Jack. So called because it only had one headlight. I do not recall it ever having two headlights.

Later, while Aunt Lurlene was cleaning up the kitchen, Uncle Spooky was reveling in his latest idea of a joke. He could hardly contain his excitement. He figured Aunt Lurlene was nervously primed for a "good un" as he would say.

As she bustled about the kitchen, Uncle Spooky went to the hall linen closet and got a pillow case. His plan was to slip out the front door, run around the house, put the pillow case over his head, run across the back porch to the window in front of the sink, yell bloody murder and frighten Aunt Lurlene.

It was a good plan… too good.

It was going well.

At the side of the house he put the pillow case over his head, and with his untied brogans hitting the ground with an awful "whoomp, whoomp, whoomp" he bounded onto the back porch.

This sudden intrusion scared the dickens out of his four sleeping dogs and they attacked. Such snarling, barking and growling you have never heard. Uncle Spooky was yelling at the top of his lungs and fighting off his dogs.

Aunt Lurlene began running around the kitchen, waving her hands and screaming hysterically.

Uncle Spooky was bitten once on the leg, once on the arm and once on the butt as he tried to retreat. His retreat was made perfect when he turned to run, and a hanging flower pot of geraniums hit him in the head causing a big gash and a lot of blood. Now he really looked bad.

Their neighbor, Otis, heard the horrible screams, yelling, barking and growling, and after calling the sheriff, grabbed his shotgun and started running toward Uncle Spooky's house. Otis began firing his shotgun into the air, so the interlopers would know more help was on the way for Spooky. This put the dogs into a total frenzied madness.

When the sheriff arrived, he saw Uncle Spooky in his headlights fighting off dogs, the bloody pillow case over his head, now decorated with geraniums, and the neighbor with his shotgun. The sheriff thought there was a feud. He and his deputy pulled their guns and waded into the fray. The deputy was bitten on the back of his leg, and the sheriff was knocked down as the deputy tried to escape the dogs. The sheriff's gun discharged and blew out the driver's side window of the patrol car.

The sheriff and his deputy began firing in the air to command attention. They got it.

With the gunshots Aunt Lurlene fainted while trying to put the green Jell-O into the refrigerator. She was now lying face down in the green gelatin.

Suddenly, there was silence…deathly, eerie silence. No screams, no barking, no gunshots, no yelling…just quiet.

The deputy put Uncle Spooky and Otis in the patrol car and the sheriff went to check on Aunt Lurlene.

Earlier Aunt Lurlene had locked the doors so the sheriff had to break in to help her. He slid down in the green gunk, now melting and covering the black and white linoleum floor, ruined his pants and got his newly polished shoes really messed up. But with the stalwart heart and bravery of a good lawman, he managed to regain his footing and help Aunt Lurlene to a chair. He got her a cool, wet cloth for her head and one for his shoes.

Meanwhile, the deputy took Uncle Spooky and himself to the emergency room. Otis went home.

I do believe if Uncle Spooky had not gone with the deputy, Aunt Lurlene would have killed him right there. She was mad as a brindle cow for weeks. Uncle Spooky stayed out of arms reach and on his very best behavior.

Aunt Lurlene did get a new car, a new wardrobe and she and Agnes took a two week vacation trip to Biloxi. They stayed at a big, fine beach front hotel and had room service and everything. They didn't have to make the beds or nothing.

They shopped just like other tourist. They bought big, garish straw hats, and matching purses that had "BILOXI" woven in hot pink yarn on the side, and the biggest, gaudiest sunglass ever made. They had a wonderful time.

Uncle Spooky stayed home.

This joke so backfired on Uncle Spooky that it ended his stupid practical jokes.

Every once in a while a little gleam appears in

his eyes, but then he rubs the scar on his head and thinks better of his idea.

A word to the wise is usually sufficient…some have to learn the hard way.

Peanuts

A "Fraidy" Hole for Little Mama

Jo Mavis and Sadie Ruth were sisters, very close sisters. They both worked for the Meridian Shirt Factory, rode to work together, ate lunch together, went to church together and raised their families together.

They took care of their mother, Little Mama. She was their special love. Little Mama was about 4'8" and weighted about eighty-five pounds. She lived alone and was quite spry for her eighty-five years. The family loved her very much.

Little Mama gave up driving and gave her car to her grandson, Billy Earl. She hasn't driven since the day she missed her driveway, ran over the mailbox, drove through the verbena bed and chased the neighbor's cat up the oak tree. It looked like she was trying to climb the tree with her car. No one knows exactly what happened, and the cat is not telling. The cat is just thankful it had more than one life. Little Mama agreed with the family to not drive again.

It was now spring of the year in Mississippi, and bad weather had a tendency to drop in and dance around on a whim. Tornados had been popping about and Jo Mavis and Sadie Ruth were concerned for Little Mama's safety. Knowing she lived across town from them didn't give them much comfort.

One day at lunch Jo Mavis said, "Sadie Ruth, our kids and husbands know what to do in case of bad weather, but what about Little Mama?"

"Well, a cellar will not help. She could not lift the door. Let's all put our heads together and see if we can find a place inside the house."

The sisters agreed. Saturday was announced as "Fraidy Hole Day." The title was provided by Jo Mavis' husband, Carl Dean. Plans were made and success would be theirs. They would find a safe place for Little Mama.

Saturday, after the dusting, vacuuming, and the weekly trip to the A & P, the family began the quest for Little Mama's 'fraidy hole. They considered the pantry, two unused bedrooms, and several closets to no avail. Finally, they were standing in front of an unused storage closet in the hall. It was about six feet long and three feet wide, with many storage shelves. At one time it was a blanket closet. It had become a catch-all for many years and now it was a time capsule.

"My word," said Jo Mavis, "this has not been opened since the war."

"Which one?" giggled Sadie Ruth.

"Civil." Little Mama answered, coming down the hall.

The afternoon was spent removing shelves, very outdated Progressive Farmer magazines (that had been saved for the dress patterns), old breakable phonograph records, several brown corsages, faded photos and numerous antique blankets and quilts. The family worked until nothing remained but the faint smell of mothballs.

Carl Dean and Billy Roy built a wide bench the length of the closet. Little Mama could just sit or lie down, turn on the flashlight, close the door and be in a safe place.

After an afternoon of work the 'fraidy hole was ready. The sisters looked with great pride and much comfort on the finished project. It was supplied with a transistor radio, books, magazines, pillows, blanket, flashlight, extra batteries, water and snacks (which had to be replenished weekly because Little

Mama ate them when no one was there).

"Well, Little Mama, you are now safe from harm. If you hear sirens, get inside, close the door and stay until someone comes." Sadie Ruth said.

"This is a safe place. The only thing you do not have is a helmet." Jo Mavis added.

Everyone laughed.

The sisters left with peace of mind for their mother's protection.

Life went on.

It was a perfect spring until around Easter. The warm Gulf air and the cold north air collated, and the sirens wailed. Everyone took cover.

It was dark as midnight when the tornado hit the southeast edge of the city. High winds, hail, heavy rains and flying debris caused great concern. As soon as the "all clear" was sounded Sadie Ruth, Jo Mavis and families hurried to Little Mama's home.

Her house had been hit. The carport was gone, part of the roof was gone and several windows were broken. Everyone began calling to Little Mama.

Suddenly, they stopped and looked at each other…they heard singing. They jerked open the door of the 'fraidy hole. There sat Little Mama with her Bible in her lap, her hands folded in prayer and singing in her wavering, elderly voice:

*"Hold me fast, let me stand in the hollow of Thy hand.
Keep me safe till the storm passes by."*

"Little Mama!" the sisters said in unison, opening the closet door.

Little Mama jumped, batted her watery blue eyes and said "I knew you would come, Sweeties."

"Are you alright?" Sadie Ruth asked.

"Oh, yes." Little Mama answered, as the girls helped her out of the closet.

"Mama," Jo Mavis said, staring at Little Mama's head, "what in the world do you have on your head?"

"Oh, that, well, you said I had everything but a helmet, so when the sirens started I grabbed my Bible, and Mama's old blue and white speckled, enamel colander and put it on my head. It worked fine." The colander was setting askew on her head. She straightened it and did a slow little shuffle dance. Pausing to look around Little Mama shook her head and said, "You girls have a real mess to clean up Saturday."

Everyone lost it. They all laughed hysterically and cried tears of relief and joy

Little Mama was fine, life was good, and God had answered all of their prayers.

Uncle Earl and Uncle Abner

Uncle Earl and Uncle Abner were brothers. They had always been good buddies. When they were kids they were always pulling pranks on each other. As the years moved on, and they grew older, the pranks of old just became stories to tell at family gatherings.

Now, Uncle Earl was a big man. I mean *BIG*. He was about 6'3" and weighed about 300 pounds. As large as he was, he was "skert" (scared) of snakes. I do mean *ter-ree-fied!* He didn't even like a crooked extension cord.

Uncle Abner was about 5' 8" and weighed about 160 pounds. He was not afraid of anything but Aunt Maudie.

One day Uncle Abner got it in his head to have some fun out of Uncle Earl. He had to go to the feed store, so he went by Uncle Earl's place and asked him to come with him. Uncle Earl liked to catch up on the latest community news (gossip) so he decided to ride along.

Uncle Earl had to get into Uncle Abner's truck on the driver's side. This took real effort. The passenger's side door would not open due to the fact that Uncle Abner's bull had rammed it last fall. Anyway, after much pushing, shoving, moaning and groaning, Uncle Earl finally got in and off they went.

Now unbeknownst to Uncle Earl, Uncle Abner had put a little grass snake in the glove box.

On down the road Uncle Abner acted like he thought he had a flat tire. He stopped, got out and walked around the truck, kicking the tires and pretending to check them real good. When he got to the passenger side window he said, "Earl, hand me that tire gage in the glove box."

Uncle Earl obliged. When the glove box lid dropped down, so did the little, bug-eyed snake. It wiggled off the lid, across Uncle Earl's knee and over to the driver's side of the truck.

Uncle Abner jes' don't know exactly how it happened, but he said before he could turn around Uncle Earl was out of the truck, fifty yards up in a field, jumpin' up and down and screamin' like a woman. The passenger door was standin' wide open, the glove box door was gone, so was the rearview mirror, the gear shift knob and the little snake. My…my…my.

Uncle Earl may have been afraid of snakes, but after that episode Uncle Abner was afraid of Uncle Earl. Verrrrry afraid!

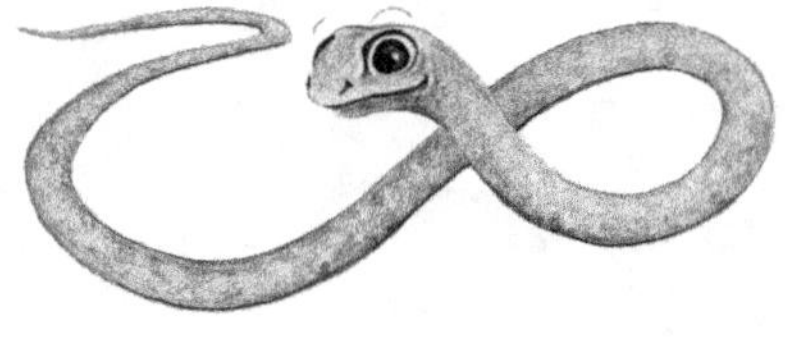

Audette and the Chicken Snake

Before I begin this story I would like to explain something to those of you who are not familiar with the chicken snake. This creepy crawler is neither a "chicken" nor a coward. It just means this snake likes little chicks, birds and eggs of any kind. This snake grows very large, is not poisonous and will not hurt you. They have, on occasion, caused many people to hurt themselves. Panic can do strange things.

And now the story…

My city cousin Audette loved visiting us on the farm. The feeling was mutual. She was one of my favorite cousins and one of the funniest people you could have ever met. Her visits were never dull.

One of Audette's favorite farm chores was to gather eggs when she visited. She would begin midmorning asking Mama if it was time to gather the eggs. Mama always gathered eggs about middle of the afternoon, after she was sure the hens had finished laying for the day.

On this particular day Audette had asked and asked and asked. Finally Mama said. "Audette, here is the egg basket. Go and gather the eggs." Audette grabbed the basket, raced across the yard to the chicken house, and began her favorite chore… gatherin' eggs.

When you entered the hen house the nests were attached to the inside front wall to the immediate right of the door. There were about six feet of nests each being 12" x 12." Each nest had hay so the eggs would not be damaged. On the back wall, opposite the nests were six or seven roosting poles. These were long poles that ran the length of the hen house and were placed in a leaning ladder fashion so the chickens could roost at night.

Enters Audette happily gathering eggs. She would run her hand into each nest, retrieve the wonderful treasure, and carefully place them in the basket. At the last nest she did the same thing, not realizing the egg she was retrieving was, at the same time, being swallowed by a very large chicken snake. When she grasped the egg she spied the snake. She jerked her arm back so fast she jerked the snake out of the nest, still attached to the egg. The panicked snake, flailing wildly, was trying to get free of the egg when he became airborne. He had never flown before. His flight came to a sudden stop as he collided with a roosting pole.

The snake was no more panicked than Audette. There are no words for what she did. She ricocheted off every wall in the hen house several times. Screaming wildly in several octaves, high and low. She tore down the roosting poles and tore the nests off the wall while trying to find the door. It was mayhem! A cloud of chicken feathers filled the air as chickens were flying, running and squawking all over the chicken yard. The dogs were barking and chasing the chickens. Audette was hitting high notes that had never been recorded before.

Mama heard Audette and was running and screaming to the rescue.

Audette broke all the eggs in the basket, plus stomping the basket flat, while screeching her way out the door to be rescued by flying into the arms of Mama! We never knew if she flung the eggs, or in her panic just stomped on them. But boy, what a sight it was!

The hen house was a disaster! Everything was

destroyed…totally destroyed. The walls were all that remained.

The hens quit laying for nearly a week.

We never found the snake.

Audette never asked to gather eggs again.

I told you it was exciting when Audette came to visit. Now you know why she was one of my favorite cousins.

So much for the peace and quiet of country life.

The Night the Rollaway Bed Ate Alvin

After the mail carrier, Mr. Long, had passed by, Mama eagerly read her letter from Aunt Sadie. Laying the letter on her lap, she clapped her hands and began laughing. "Kids, Sadie and Alvin are coming tomorrow, for a few days. It will be wonderful to see them. Now we must tidy the house."

Then began the *tidyin'* assignments:

"Robert E. Lee take out the trash and burn it. Boone get the brush broom and sweep the yard. Eli put the rollaway bed on the screened-in back porch for Alvin. Shake out the cushions on the wicker settee, and you can sleep out there with him. Gladys Ann dust the furniture, and sweep and mop the living room. I will fry up some chicken, make a cake and change the sheets on the beds. Now let's get busy!"

Everyone scattered to their respective duties. Mama's orders were never met with any argument. They were akin to Moses receiving the Ten Commandments. There was just no discussion.

The next day we could hardly wait for our company to arrive. We all loved Aunt Sadie and her family very much. We loved Alvin, but sometimes he could be a real pill. He was very smart and excelled in everything he did, but he was a city boy, *deeluxe*. After all, he was from downtown Hattiesburg, and we were country cousins who lived three miles on a red clay road near Collinsville, Mississippi. His daddy worked for Sears and Roebuck, and our daddy was a construction worker and farmed with our grandpa. Still we were always happy to see him come and happier to see him go.

We were very excited when we saw the big, blue Hudson turn into our yard. We were squealin' and jumpin' around, huggin' and all talkin at the same time.

Mama and Aunt Sadie were cryin' and huggin' like they had not seen each other in years. Theirs was always a tearful, joyous reunion and their departure was just the same…well, tearful, at least.

Alvin enjoyed the farm. He followed me to gather the eggs and went to the barn when Daddy

milked the cows. He chased chickens, and picked
green apples, and played with the boys in a game of
country jig (a sorta baseball game…usually played
when there were not near enough players for a real
game). Alvin tried, although he could not hit a ball
the size of a milk bucket. He loved to play.

After supper, while Alvin and Eli chased
lightning bugs through the potato patch, Robert E.
and I sat on the front porch steps listening to the
adults talk. They told stories we had heard before,
but they grew better with each telling.

As the evening grew darker, the stories became
spookier. By now, everyone was sitting on the porch
and steps listening as Papa began his story about
Uncle Ezra and his prize winning hog, Hazel.

Now, let me explain… Hazel had never won a
prize, nor had she ever been entered into any contest.
Uncle Ezra always just called her "Hazel, the prize
winning hawg." Hazel weighted about 500 pounds
and slept in front of Uncle Ezra's fireplace in winter
and on the front porch in summer.

Papa's story began. "Now this is the story Uncle
Ezra told me. Uncle Ezra told it this way.

On this particular hot Mississippi evening Uncle
Ezra was nipping a little too much when he went
into the barn to milk the cows. He left the hog pen

gate open, so Hazel decided to take a walk to the creek and cool off. When Uncle Ezra realized where she was headed, he took in after her (that means he chased her).

Uncle Ezra was calling, beggin', pleadin' and even singin' her favorite songs, but Hazel only responded with an occasional oink and never looked back."

Papa paused a moment for the perfect effect, widened his eyes, and said softly, "It was gettin' reeely dark."

Caught up in the story, hardly anyone breathed. I tell you, it was very quiet on that front porch.

Now, using Uncle Ezra's twangy voice, Papa proceeded. "Hazel continued to squeal and run. When she got to the creek she just plowed right into the water. She rolled and turned and splashed just like she was in heaven. Uncle Ezra got closer, and tossed her an ear of corn. He was singin' softly, "Come on, pretty Hazel. Come on, pretty girl." Hazel paused for a moment, yielded to temptation, and started for the corn. She was almost at the edge of the creek when Uncle Ezra said, "sumpum big as a gorilla riz up 'bout eight feet out of that creek, grabbed Hazel's back legs and drug her back into the water. It was huge…and black…and ugly. It drug

Hazel down into the water and disappeared back into the creek."

Everyone gasped.

The saga goes on…

"Uncle Ezra was sho 'nuff scared. He ran all the way home, screamin,' and hollorin', and cryin' and takin' on.   Nothin' of Hazel, the prize winning hog, was ever found anywhere up and down that creek bank. Sunday morning, however, did find Uncle Ezra at church, sober and singin' loud in the front pew." (Religion does have a way of making one feel safe. Most folks know where to go when the world gets too rough.)

It was very silent on the front porch when Mama said, "Hush up, Josh. You gonna give these kids bad dreams." Then she said, "You kids get ready for bed now."

Alvin whined and pouted about having to sleep on the rollaway bed. He threw a fit, a real hissy fit, kicked covers, and flounced about until Aunt Sadie went out and sat with him. He finally dozed off to sleep.

After all us kids were bedded down, Papa, Mama and Aunt Sadie moved to the kitchen table for more sweet tea and conversation.

After about two hours of their visiting, the night was shattered (no, that's not the word), it was more like a large rip in the universe. The shrill, electrical shriek was loud, and without loss of volume, became muffled. It never ceased. It just changed intensity, loud…muffled…loud…muffled, and then there was a resounding crash. (No, that, too, is not accurate.) There was a crash, a skid, a thud and boom. The sheets, blanket and pillow were dragging, flopping and flying. The roll-away bed was on the loose!

Although Eli had moaned about having to sleep on the settee, he now realized he had the best seat in the house for this event. He was jumping up and down on the wicker settee and laughing his head off. He was yelling, "Ride 'em, Alvin, ride 'em." Eli offered no assistance. He was impressed with Alvin's ability to stay with the monster for the full ride.

Papa, Mama and Aunt Sadie, instant in their response, arrived to see this rollicking rodeo. With Alvin screaming "It's got me…it's got me. It ate Hazel, and now it's got me."

The three adults immediately began chasing this bounding sheet and striped ticking monster. After several near misses and Aunt Sadie falling on her fanny, Papa finally cornered the rogue monster, and the bed just gave up, listed to one side, and lay over on it's side in surrender. Alvin was still screaming… muffled, but screaming, between the folds of the mattress.

Papa quickly righted the bed and removed Alvin, who, although shaking like a leaf, promptly announced he had not been afraid.

Alvin did get his way. He did not have to sleep on the rollaway bed. The rest of their visit he slept on a pallet in the hall.

Be warned…those rollaway beds are sneaky. They can be aggressive and attack without warning.

Govner, the Blood Hound

It is common knowledge in the South that you can steal a man's wife, but do not take his huntin' dog or his pick-up truck. These men do love their huntin' dogs.

Well, Uncle Clyde had a slow, real lazy ol' hound dog named Govner. Uncle Clyde loved Govner. Govner was not very good at hunting, but Uncle Clyde finally trained him to hunt, point, and fetch. Although Govner was unimpressed with the whole procedure, he loved Uncle Clyde and was happy to have his attention.

Things was goin' along pretty good until Govner started chasing cars. For some reason Govner just loved that little bright green Volkswagen of Miss Helen Joiner. It became a daily battle between Govner and the green thing. When nearing Uncle Clyde's house you could hear that little car begin to whine as Miss Joiner began to pick up speed so she could out run Govner.

One day she just was not fast enough. Govner scared the life out of her when he jumped in the window of her Volkswagen. She screamed like a banshee, ran off the road, bumped her head on the steering wheel, lost her glasses and ruined the little spring flowers on her beautiful Sears and Roebuck Easter hat "from their Spring Collection."

Uncle Clyde was very sorry and was glad to fix her car, buy her new glasses, and replace her beautiful Sears and Roebuck Easter hat.

After that, Uncle Clyde kept Govner tied with a big rope to the big oak in the front yard.

One lovely spring day it came up a sudden rain storm. The lightning flashed and the thunder rumbled something fierce. Uncle Clyde wasn't home so poor Govner was left to the elements.

During the storm the lightning struck near the big oak. The electricity ran through the tree and whomped the dickens out of Govner. Thanks to the rope and leather collar Govner did not get the full jolt.

Uncle Clyde was quite shaken over Govner's close call.

Govner was laid up for quite a spell, but with

Uncle Clyde feeding him Southern fried chicken, fresh butter beans and pecan pie every day, he did get better and fat.

But poor Govner was never right after that. He was cross eyed, which made for some very interesting hunts. He saw two of everything and the decision of which direction to point was just too strenuous. Also, the lightning left his balance a bit off. When he would raise his front leg for the point, he would fall over and Uncle Clyde would have to set him back on his feet.

Uncle Clyde felt so guilty about what had happened to Govner, he never tied him up again. Every day Uncle Clyde took him to the Dairy Queen and bought him ice cream. Govner was one happy dog and when Govner was happy Uncle Clyde was happy.

Miss Joiner was safe because Govner was never sure of which window to jump into. After running into the side of the car a couple of times, he finally gave up chasing her car.

Govner lived a long and happy life.

Napoleon

Let me tell you about Napoleon. You see, this little general marched around the yard in full regalia every day. No one questioned his authority. Napoleon was a banty rooster (I think the proper name was Bantam). As a chick he had been stepped on by Bob, my grandpa's horse. That day we thought Napoleon was a goner for sure, but he proved his resilience…he lived. After the accident, he did not walk like a chicken. He walked upright. He really did not walk, he marched, a very aristocratic march. Napoleon would ruffle his neck feathers and standing erect as he did he looked like he was wearing a headdress, a very regal headdress. He struck quite a Napoleonic pose…thus his name. He was beautiful.

Napoleon was the king of the yard. Nothing… dogs, cats, other roosters, or old hens on the pecks,

challenged him. With his colorful feathers shining
in the sun he was an imposing force to be reckoned
with. And if some misguided one thought he could
usurp Napoleon's authority that would be the only
time they believed that misconception. With flying
feathers, flashing spurs and demonic shrieks he
made short order of the intruder. When the dust
settled Napoleon was still one tough little rooster in
control of his beat, the yard and the hen house.

He was such a sight that when we had visitors,
they all wanted to see Napoleon. He loved the
grains he was offered from their hands. He bobbed
up and down to retrieve the offerings, and then strike
his aristocratic pose, stand, lift his head, and march
away.

Napoleon lived to be a very old, but ever, regal
rooster. When he died we gave him a funeral fit
for any monarch. We placed his tiny, beautifully
feathered body in a shoe box we had wrapped in
red Christmas paper and lined with a soft white
cloth. Mama covered the lid with white lace from
her sewing box. His brier was the Western Flyer red
wagon we washed for the occasion.

The procession was very fine. My brothers,
George and Michael, were the drum and fife corps.
They somberly led the procession. George slowly

tapped the molasses can drum. Michael played the fife (a comb covered with waxed paper). The music of the corps was very good. Jim, my younger brother, slowly pulled the wagon as the procession followed the drum and fife corps. I, the eulogizer, followed the brier. Mother and Daddy followed respectfully behind. Sad faces all around.

After a short eulogy we sang Napoleon's favorite song, The Chicken Song, and then we buried Napoleon under the apricot tree, his favorite place. Daddy gave the benediction and the service was ended.

Napoleon had gone to that great hen house in the sky.

Long live Napoleon.

Little Bobby Bailey Gets Baptized

Now you have to know that when you grow
up in a small town in the South the church is like a
country club. The folks all gather once a week to
talk politics, crops, and to nod in agreement with
the preacher's message whether they are listening or
not.

This year was a banner event in our church.
Not only did we get running water and an indoor
bathroom in our church, we got a bran' spankin,
deeluxe, best on the market, baptistery. It had
a heater and everything. Miss Ina Mae Jenkins
painted a mural (that means a picture 'sept it don't
have a frame) on the wall behind it. It looked
like the Jordan River was pourin' right into the
baptistery. It was awesome, and we were so proud.
Of course, our pastor had graciously offered the
use of it to the Methodist Church and the Church of

God. It was the Christian thing to do.

Well, Little Bobby Bailey (that was his nickname *Little* Bobby) got saved that year in Vacation Bible School, and Preacher Snowden was most eager to use this awesome new facility. So one sweltering hot Sunday afternoon in August the baptism service was scheduled.

All Little Bobby's relatives and friends from far and near were present. They were wearing their Sunday best because of the special occasion. The men were wearing suits and ties (the one suit in their closet that was relegated for such things as funeral, wedding, and, of course, baptisms). The ladies were dressed in their navy crepe or flowerdy silk dresses and hats, large and small, decorated with flowers, birds, fruit etc.

Little Bobby was thrilled to be the first to be baptized in the new baptistery. His mama and daddy were equally thrilled. His mother kept dabbing her eyes and his daddy, a deacon, strutted around like Goliath just before he was rocked to sleep.

Access to the baptistery was gained from each end. There were two small dressing rooms at each side of the baptistery. There were four steps up from the dressing room floor to a short platform, and then steps that led down into the baptistery where the preacher was standing.

The pianist, Mrs. Pigford, began softly playing "Shall We Gather at the River" and the somber ceremony commenced.

Preacher Snowden stepped to the side of the baptistery, led the congregation in prayer and then gingerly stepped into the water. He was wearin' his new waders, purchased just for this occasion, so he could change quickly into his suit and greet the people after the ceremony.

Little Bobby, clad in his starched white shirt and creased khaki pants began his walk. From the dressing room he ascended the stairs and started across the platform. All eyes were on him.

You could hear an occasional snub in the congregation.

Suddenly, on impulse, Little Bobby hunches over and with pounding steps he increases his speed and just as he gets to the steps to descend into the water he did a cannonball into the baptistery. He came up spitting and splashing.

The preacher, trying to avoid this hurdling eight year old, steps backward, loses his footing and disappears from the congregation's view. His waders fill with water, and it is a real struggle for him to regain his footing, but by holding on to the side of the baptistery he is finally in standing position.

There was an instant tsunami on the Jordan River. It looked like the river was running upstream. Most of the water was knocked out of the baptistery. It was all over the podium and the first three rows in the congregation. Everyone was blessed with an impromptu sprinkling of holy water. This was all right with the Methodists who were visiting.

Uncle Rufus' wool suit began to shrink and some of the crepe dresses began to pucker. All the ladies hats were well watered.

Pastor Snowden regained his composure and completed the baptism. Several of the men had to help him out of the baptistery because with the filled waders he could not get up the steps. He looked like he had gained fifty pounds. The men had to pull the curtain for the pastor to remain descent and to help him out of his waders. This could have given a whole new meaning to the expression "southern exposure."

It was nice to hear "amens" and "hallelujahs" all around.

Little Bobby did not think about heaven for a while. Immediately following the baptism Bobby's dad carried him, by the shirt collar, dripping wet,

out back for a "little talk."   Bobby caught more heat
than heaven. We could tell from the shoutin' and
bawlin' in the edge of the woods behind the church
that Little Bobby would never forget his baptism
day.

Praise!!! Praise!!! Lift your hands and shout.

A True Chicken Snake Story

The weather warms up fast in Mississippi.
Daddy decided to take several high boards off the
side of the chicken house and cover the opening
with chicken wire. This would make it cooler for
the chickens during the soon-to-be hot Mississippi
summer.

Like most of daddy's projects he followed
through with his plans, but left the remaining roll of
wire leaning against the hen house "until he could
get around to puttin' it up."

One day we kids were playing cowboys and
Indians when we saw a very, very large chicken
snake hanging lengthwise, high on the wire on the
outside of the chicken house. He was about five
feet off the ground. He had apparently climbed the
roll of wire while trying to find his way into the hen
house. I guess he just got tired and decided to take a

nap.

We took off yellin' and screamin' for Mama. I don't know how she ever figured out what this gang of yellin' kids was saying, but she calmly went back into the house and got the shotgun. This was not Mama's usual weapon of choice.

(Let me interject something here…my Mama could shoot a gun. She used a Stevens Favorite single shot .22 rifle and a nickel-plated Smith & Wesson .38 Special revolver, depending on the seriousness of impending danger, I suppose. Most of Mama's shooting was just Sunday afternoon entertainment. She could shoot the end of a corn cob and split it into three equal parts. On one occasion, with only two remaining cartridges, she lay two Coke bottles facing her on the fence, and with two shots, shot through the neck of each bottle and shot out the bottom, leaving the rest of the bottle undamaged. Another time she saw a hawk get one of her chickens. She shot the hawk with the rifle and the chicken fell back into the chicken pen. Between the hawk and the fall it was a rough day for the chicken. Like I said, my Mama could shoot a gun.)

This day, in true Annie Oakley fashion, she eased around the chicken house. It was deathly silent. No one breathed. The birds stopped singing, the chickens settled quietly to the ground and the dogs crawled, whining, under the porch. Mama put the gun up to her shoulder, took aim and fired.

The world exploded! The quiet was suddenly ruptured with a cacophony of dog barks, chicken squawks, bird shrieks, kids yelling and the universe gone completely crazy.

She killed that snake into fourteen pieces, blew three boards off the hen house and the hens quit layin' for a week.

Mama was death to snakes and hawks or any varmint that dared enter our world.

Gertie and the Christmas Pageant

Note: pageant means a spectacular exhibition. This event did not miss the true meaning of "Christmas Pageant."

Mrs. Perkins had worked long and hard to set the perfect scene for the annual Baptist Church Christmas Pageant. She took great pride in her attention to details. The script had been written many years before so she devoted every effort to create an authentic recreation of the blessed event. The pulpit had been removed to clear the stage and she had outdone herself for the setting to be as near the original as possible.

The stage was breath taking. The backdrop was sheets, dyed navy, and hung in front of the baptistery. The sheets were covered with yellow construction paper stars with the largest star, covered with aluminum foil, in the center to guide the wise men. This year Mrs. Perkins had improved on this play. She had found small bales of hay and placed them on the stage near the manger which was center stage. The setting was perfect. Risers sat in front of the "night sky" curtains for the heavenly choir to sing the appropriate carol to coincide with the narration and the on-stage action of the play.

The angelic heavenly choir's costumes were their daddy's white tee shirts, nylon net covered cardboard wings and coat hanger halos wrapped in foil. Most of which were askew, but I digress.

The wise men were to enter stage right. East, of course. Their costumes were rich colored bath robes, cardboard crowns covered with "jewels" and carrying gifts for the Baby Jesus.

The abiding shepherds, carrying their staffs and wearing men's old brown sweatshirts, turned inside out with sleeves cut off, and tea towel head dresses, would enter from stage left.

Mrs. Perkins had left no detail unattended. She had borrowed Gertie Mayett's baby doll to be the Christ child. This negotiation was made with the promise of ice cream and a solemn oath that the doll would only lay in the manger. Mary would not take it out at all. After negotiations were agreed upon, Gertie helped Mrs. Perkins wrap the baby in swaddling clothes and lay it in the manger. Even though it had blond hair and blue eyes wrapped in swaddling clothes it could almost pass for the baby Messiah. The stage was now perfect for the glorious coming event.

Mary (Claudine Vance) and Joseph (Raymond Tucker) were to sit at each end of the manger as each set of night visitors came slowly and prayerfully to the manger. Mrs. Ethel Hewitt, armed with a small flashlight, would narrate at a small podium near the piano played by Mrs. Pigford.

At last the wonderful night arrived. The church was full. Everyone tried to get as close to the front as possible, something you rarely see in a Baptist church service.

Mary and Joseph were at the manger. The heavenly choir members were in their places and the shepherds and wise men were waiting in the wings.

With the piano playing softly in the background, Mrs. Hewitt began her reading of Luke's account of the Christmas story…from the King James Version, of course.

The heavenly choir softly sang "Away in a Manger" as the story began.

With the Heavenly Herald's announcement "Fear not, for behold I bring you good tidings of great joy.

For unto you is born this day in the city of David a savior, which is Christ the Lord." the abiding shepherds were on cue to worship the King to the songs "While Shepherds Watched Their Flocks by Night" and "Angels We Have Heard on High."

To "We Three Kings" three noble wise men, bedecked in their finery and carrying gifts of gold, frankincense and myrrh came down the center aisle, turned right and mounted the steps to arrive from the east.

The program was going well. Mrs. Perkins was so pleased with all of the children. The choir was indeed heavenly and the actors were in their places perfectly. She breathed a sigh of relief. Too Soon!

Little Gertie had sat quietly watching the manger. She never took her eyes off her baby. She had been reluctant, but her mother had explained that her doll had the most important part in the play. She had finally consented, but *NOW SHE WAS NOT SURE!*

This doll was Gertie's birthday baby doll. It went everywhere with Gertie. It had never missed Sunday school, trips to town or Vacation Bible School. Gertie loved her baby.

The play was running smoothly when Mary, the holy mother of Jesus, decided to take the new born king out of the manger to cuddle him.

Gertie could not take this. In a split second she was out of her seat, bounded down the aisle, up the steps and made a headlong dash for her baby.

Mary refused to give up her new born son and the fight was on.

Only Solomon could assess this situation.

Please keep in mind this was not a skirmish. Bull Run was a skirmish.

On center stage Gertie and the Virgin were pulling and tugging and scratching and screaming and biting and pulling hair. The newborn baby was losing his swaddling clothes. Did I tell you the play was X rated?

The audience was stunned. The pastor started to interfere, but saw Gertie was an army of one and changed his mind.

The heavenly choir was singing softly "Silent Night." Mrs. Hewitt tried to continue her narration by raising her voice above the melee that was a cannon or two short of a battlefield encounter.

The manger was tipped over and hay was flying everywhere. Shepherds abandoned their shepherd's crooks and wise men lost their crowns as they all scurried to safety. Joseph, with a frozen benign smile, stood near with his staff. He was beyond stage fright. If I remember correctly he was so traumatized he had to have a Cocola and a Moon Pie after the event to calm him down.

With a final push from Gertie, The Virgin Mary landed on her rear. Gertie, and her baby doll, triumphantly left the stage and returned to her seat.

Gertie sat calmly cooing to her baby and was oblivious to everyone.

The blessed mother, with her head dress gone and her halo bent, sat and kicked and screamed until her mother arrived, and exited the stage with the Chosen One still kicking and screaming.

The heavenly choir lustily sang "Joy to the World."

The applause was deafening.

Mrs. Perkins fainted.

It was a great pageant.

It was a great Christmas.

The Play was, indeed, the thing.

About The Author...

Sue Carlton Swinson grew up in Collinsville, Mississippi, a small, rural community, where everyone knew everyone and each had a story to share.

Exposure to storytelling was everywhere: home, family reunions, school, church and community. One of her favorite times was family reunions and listening to the "grown-ups" tell stories. Wherever people got together the storytelling began. Her love for stories, books and writing emerged from these wonderfully vivid tales.

In addition to her beautiful children's stories, she has now drawn on some of the "get together" stories for her latest book *The Hen House Chronicles*. This entertaining collection is about growing up Southern and a good life "just a little left of center."

About The Illustrator...

Linda Shaw has had a lifetime career as an artist in various media. Her work appears across the country. In recent years she has illustrated a number of children's books. She finds it challenging and rewarding to transform the writer's vision into images which delight and stimulate the young reader.

Children's Books

By

Sue Carlton Swinson

McMortie, a little gray mouse, forgets his mother's
instrucitons and goes in search of his favorite food...
tea cakes. You will love the excitement of reading about
McMortie's great adventure

McMortie loves baseball. He also loves to win. In his latest
adventure McMortie learns the true meaning of freindship,
teamwork and how to be a real winner.

McMortie, the little grey mouse, is very excited when a hot
air balloon lands in the meadow near his home. He just
has to get a closer look at the balloon. McMortie forgets to
listen to Uncle Herman's instructions and finds himself in
the middle of another great adventure. This story is exciting
from start to finish. Read and enjoy the great adventure and
the happy ending.

Do you believe that a little pig can become a frog, a bird, or a butterfly? Well, enjoy this story as Willie Pig tries to become somthing he is not. Willie Pig learns a valuable lesson when he finally listens to his friends who tell him, "Be the best little pig you can be and not a Silly Willie Pig.

Enjoy this magical story about a wonderful little dragon and his best friend Huan. The beautiful setting of this story stirs the imagination as Zhang and Huan learn that being with those you love brings a special happiness. Discover why Zhang really is "the little dragon of happiness."

Come and soar with North Wind on a very special Christmas adventure. North Wind with the help of thousands of beautiful butterflies brings special joy to a family at Christmas time. This delightful Christmas story will capture the imaginations of children of all ages. They will soon know what makes North Wind's heart "very, very, VERY happy."

Baxter, a little brown caterpillar, admires al the brightly colored insects in the garden. Read the story and learn how the magic of believing in the Awesome One changed Baxter from a little, fat, brown worm to a spectacular blue butterfly.

Sue Carlton Swinson | P.O. Box 93194 | Lubbock, TX 79493 | 806-470-5095 | 806-791-3741